BEAR WITH ME

MAX KORNELL

SCHOLASTIC INC.

For Psipsina, Ajax and Ramona.
I love you all very much.

It started off just right. I had a mom
and a dad and my own set of blocks.
I had everything I needed.

Then one day my mom and dad brought home a surprise. I don't like surprises. Surprises are never as good as you hoped for.

They said they always wanted a bear.
They said now the family was complete.
I thought the family was already complete.
The bear's name was Gary.

I told my mom and dad that they should
have asked me if I wanted a bear. If they
had asked, they would have known that
I don't want a bear.

They said **Gary** was going to sleep in my room.
They said **Gary** gets to use all my toys.
I said I don't like sharing.
What if he breaks my stuff? . . .
They said, That's the way it is now.

Later, I asked my mom to take me to the park to fly my kite. She said Not right now because she had to take Gary for a walk.

I asked my dad to build a block castle with me, but he said
Not right now because he had to put together Gary's
new bed before bedtime. He did not even ask me to help.

Gary's snores are so loud that it sounds like there is a helicopter flying around in circles in my room.

Gary forgets to put
the caps back on
my markers.

Gary broke the swing
in the backyard.

I said

This stinks!

. . . to nobody.

It turns out **Gary** is really
good with blocks.

He knows how to make things fit just right.

Gary even showed me
how we could still
use the swing.

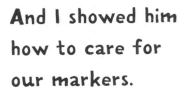

And I showed him
how to care for
our markers.

Maybe surprises are not so bad.

Some surprises turn out even
better than you hoped for.